MW00891042

"The animals in this faraway place loved their home. Most of the time, it was a wonderful place to live. The trees were full of fruit to eat and the streams and rivers flowed with cool fresh water to drink. But one year it didn't rain, not one little drop, not for months and months! So nothing grew and the faraway place was no longer such a wonderful place to live."

"Each and every animal was hungry, even big, fierce Tiger. 'Grrrr!' she growled, and so did her stomach as she prowled. She was looking for something—*anything*—to eat. That's when she spied some dried-up old yams. The yams were small and shriveled because the land was so dry. 'Those yams don't look too tasty,' Tiger said to herself. 'But I'm hungry enough to eat them anyhow.' So she started to dig.

"The yams were waiting for rain, though, and didn't want to come out of the ground. The more Tiger dug, the angrier the yams became. In fact, they were so angry they came alive!"

"Those yams jumped up and began to chase Tiger away. And the sound of their dried-up legs on the ground was *boom boom ticky-picky, boom boom ticky-picky.*

'Help!' yelled Tiger. 'Somebody save me from the yams!' But the sight of that big, fierce tiger being chased by those little tiny yams just made the other animals laugh."

"Not one of those animals would help. Tiger ran and the yams chased, *boom boom ticky-picky*, until Goat came along. Kind, brave Goat caught each one of those yams on his horns! That night, he and Tiger had a feast while the other animals stayed hungry out in the dark. And even shriveled up, those yams tasted delicious!

"Nevertheless, for all the rest of her life, Tiger could not see a yam without hearing the sound *boom boom ticky-picky, boom boom ticky-picky, boom boom ticky-picky. . . .*"

Can you see the other animals?

Next Vanessa told a spooky tale.
"Once there was a girl who believed in witches, but her father did not. So the girl said,
'Daddy, you'll see—I'll catch a real live witch!'
'How will you do that?' asked her father.
'Easy! I'll lay a witch trap! I'll sprinkle salt under a sifter and leave it out all night long!'"

"The father laughed. He didn't believe his little girl would catch *anything*, let alone a witch. But besides knowing all about witches, she knew about bugs and creepy crawly things, including the fact that all of them love to eat salt. So that night the girl and her little brother snuck in and laid the witch trap right beside their father's bed."

Can you see the salt?

"Just at midnight the girl and her brother heard a strange noise in their father's room. *Rackety rack, rackety rack.* The sifter was moving!

'What's that under there?' their father asked, and he was mighty nervous.

'It's a witch, of course,' said the little girl.

'Yowee!' The father jumped up in bed, then he plucked the sifter up. 'Hmph! That's no witch.'

'Oh, yes it is,' said the little girl, laughing. 'Witches can turn into anything they please!'

Then even her daddy laughed. 'Okay, you got me this time. Your witch trap really worked!'"

Can you see what they caught?

"Your story was funny *and* scary, Vanessa," says Shaina. "But mine is even scarier! Once upon a time—"

"Wait," says James. "That sounds like the beginning of a *fairy* tale, not a *scary* tale!"

"James, just listen and you'll see," says Shaina. "One time a family went camping, and they got frightened because while they were sitting around, all the spooky night animals came—"

"You're not scaring *me*," James says.

"Then what's in that tree behind you?" asks Shaina. "What's that scary noise?"

"Which tree?" asks James. "What noise?"

"Shaina, you're seeing things!" Vanessa says.
"I sure am!" says Shaina. "Look! There's something over Daddy's head!"
"Where?" asks Miss Natalie.
"What?" asks Mr. Ron.
"Boo!" says Shaina.

All the Alstons are spooked now, except Shaina! What is everybody seeing?

"Shaina, you sure had me going!" says Mr. Ron. "I wonder whether my story will scare everyone. It's a ghost story."

"Tell it and we'll see!" Miss Natalie says.

"Okay, here goes," says Mr. Ron. "In olden times a girl and her father found a broken-down house where no one lived. Inside, all covered with dust, were a rocking chair and a pair of beautiful blue shoes. The girl tried on the shoes and they fit just right. But when she touched the rocker it made a terrible noise. Can you hear it? *Scritch scritch, scritch scritch!*"

"Back at home, the girl put the rocker on the porch and the beautiful shoes under her bed. Then she went to sleep. But in the deep silence of the middle of the night she woke up. Something was going *scritch scritch, scritch scritch*."

"The girl leaped out of bed and ran to the porch. But no one was in the chair! 'Who are you? Where are you?' she whispered.

'It's me and I'm going away,' a voice whispered back. 'I've been trapped in that dusty old house for a hundred years! Thank you for setting me free!'"

Can you see who was talking?

"Daddy, your story only scared me a little bit," says Shaina.

"Do you want to be scared a lot?" asks James. "Then listen to this—did any of you ever hear of the Hiccuping Monster?"

"Not me," says Miss Natalie.

"Or me," says Mr. Ron.

"Me neither," says Shaina. "But I know one thing—monsters are scary!"

"Not all monsters are scary," says Vanessa.

"Well, this one is!" says James. "Long ago this monster had the hiccups, and no matter what he did he couldn't get rid of them. Now, every time he hiccups—"

Suddenly there is a noise in the trees.

"What was that?" whispers Shaina.

"It's the Hiccuping Monster—run!" shrieks Vanessa.
But it's only Binyah Binyah Pollywog!
Everyone shouts, "You scared us, Binyah Binyah!"
"Heh, heh!" he laughs. They all help clean him off.
"James," says Vanessa, "did you ever actually hear the Hiccuping Monster?"

"Not really," James says. "But I think he might sound something like—"
"Croooakk!" says Binyah Binyah.
"That's it, Binyah!" says James. "And if the real monster comes around here, we'll get you to scare him away!"